Cody Smith and the Holiday Mysteries

(A Cody Smith Mystery)

by Dorothy Francis

Perfection Learning®

Cover and Inside Illustrations: William Ersland

About the Author

Dorothy Francis has written many books and stories for children and adults.

Ms. Francis holds a bachelor of music degree from the University of Kansas. She has traveled with an all-girl dance band, taught music in public and private schools, and served as a correspondence teacher for the Institute of Children's Literature in Connecticut.

She and her husband, Richard, divide their time between Marshalltown, Iowa, and Big Pine Key, Florida.

Text © 2001 by Perfection Learning® Corporation.

Printed in the United States of America. For information, contact

Perfection Learning® Corporation

1000 North Second Avenue, P.O. Box 500

Logan, Iowa 51546-0500

Phone: 1-800-831-4190 • Fax: 1-712-644-2392

Paperback ISBN 0-7891-5382-3

Cover Craft® ISBN 0-7807-9743-4

Printed in the U.S.A.

4 5 6 7 8 PP 10 09 08 07 06

Table of Contents

Cody Smith and the Holiday Mysteries

Featuring Cody Smith and Maria Romero

Introduction

Cody Smith and Maria Romero are friends. They are also detectives. They like to solve mysteries together.

Cody's mom is a store detective. Cody admires her a lot. When he grows up, Cody hopes to be a detective like his mom.

Cody has made several attempts to become famous. He dreams of being in the *Guinness Book of World Records*. He imagines his name on a historical marker or his face on a postage stamp. Becoming an eponym is another one of his goals. But none of these attempts at fame has been successful yet.

Cody hopes that fame will bring a call or visit from Dad. He misses his dad, who left the family.

Maria is staying with the Smiths. Her parents are working in Italy temporarily. Besides being a detective, Maria wants to be a news reporter. Someday she plans to write a book. Sometimes she even writes stories about the mysteries she and Cody solve.

Mom's detective work is often hard to find. So the Smiths move a lot. Cody and Maria find mysteries to solve wherever they are living. Right now their home is in Cottonwood, Kansas.

Cody and Maria have already solved two mysteries in Cottonwood. They have made a name for themselves around town. How many more mysteries await the detective duo?

1

The Case of the Slippery Sled

A New Year's Mystery

Cody stamped snow from his boots. His breath looked like cotton candy in the air. So did Maria's. Cody liked to feel cold air in his lungs. He liked its clean smell.

Today was New Year's Day. Was this how a new year always smelled? Cody wondered. But he couldn't remember.

Maria liked winter too. She ate cinnamon balls to keep her mouth warm. And usually she shared them with Cody.

Both Cody and Maria liked to be outside in the snow. They had lived in Cottonwood, Kansas, only a few months. This was the first big snowfall since they had moved there.

Yesterday, a foot of fresh snow had fallen in Cottonwood. Now people rushed outside with snow shovels. Some neighborhood kids laughed and threw snowballs. Others caught snowflakes on their tongues.

Maria wore her radio headphones. She wore them a lot. Today she heard an important announcement. She shared the news with Cody.

"Cottonwood kids are holding a sled race," Maria said. "It'll be at Carter's Hill. And it's going to start at 2:00."

"I don't think I'll enter the race," Cody said. "My sled's too old. It's hard to steer it in a straight line."

"I won't enter either," Maria said. "I don't even have a sled. But Carter's Hill is close by. Let's go and watch our friends race."

Cody and Maria headed down the block. They stopped when they saw four kids near Rick's house. Dan, Julie, and Jamal stood arguing with Rick.

"It's The Three 'Mouthketeers,' " Cody said.

"Who?" Maria asked.

"Dan, Julie, and Jamal," Cody replied. "I've nicknamed them."

Maria laughed. "You always like to nickname people. But why such a strange nickname?"

"I think it really fits them," Cody said. "They live in the same neighborhood. They hang out together after school. And all three started wearing braces this month."

"Guess it is a good nickname," Maria agreed.

"And they've taken a solemn vow," Cody said. "They promised one another to avoid sticky treats. At least until the braces come off."

"Look," Maria said. "Rick's motioning to us. He wants us to come over. What do you suppose is going on?"

"Let's go see," Cody said.

Cody and Maria waited until the snowplow passed. Then they crossed the snow-packed street.

"What's up?" Cody asked the kids.

"You two are good at solving mysteries," Rick said. "See if you can untangle this one."

Cody grinned. He liked to be known as a detective. He might have been new in town. But kids already knew about him.

"We'll try to help you," Maria said. "Tell us about this mystery. Start right from the beginning."

Rick took a deep breath and began. "Today's the sled race on Carter's Hill. I planned to enter. It starts less than an hour from now. I don't want to be late. Latecomers are disqualified."

"I heard that you won that race last year," Maria said.

"Yes, that's right," Rick said. "And I want to try to win again this year. The merchants are furnishing prizes. First prize is a pair of ice skates. I've never owned ice skates. Second prize is a stocking cap in school colors. I'd like that too."

"So what's happened?" Cody asked.

"I started toward Carter's Hill," Rick said. "Then I came back. I'd forgotten my gloves. So I ran inside to get them. Of course I didn't take my sled inside with me. Mom doesn't allow that. I left the sled right here in front of my house. I thought it would be safe.

"I wasn't gone over five minutes. When I returned, Dan and Jamal were here. Julie was running toward my house. But my sled was missing. It's gone. I think one of them took it. But I can't figure out which one."

"What do you have to say about this, Mouthketeers?" Maria asked. "Did one of you take Rick's sled?"

Nobody answered. Dan kicked at some snow with his toe. Julie jammed her hands into her pockets. Jamal pulled his stocking cap lower over his ears. All three of them scowled.

At last, Cody spoke up. "Jamal, I know you broke

your sled last week. Did you decide to borrow Rick's sled without asking?"

"Don't try to blame me," Jamal said. "I was just walking by. I saw Dan in front of Rick's house. And I saw Julie across the street. But I didn't see Rick's sled."

"Julie?" Maria asked. "What about you? You told me you'd rather ice-skate than go sledding. Have you changed your mind? The radio announcer made the race sound like fun. Did you decide to enter the race after all? Were you planning to use Rick's sled?"

"No fair blaming me," Julie said. "I was returning home from the library. I didn't see Rick's sled. And I didn't see Rick either. So I ran home for some bubble gum. Then I looked out the window and saw Rick and Dan. I came over to wish Rick luck. But the boys were arguing."

"Did you see Rick's sled, Dan?" Cody asked. "You entered the race last year, didn't you?"

"Yes," Dan said. "But my sled runners weren't much good. So I didn't win. I haven't gotten new ones yet. So I didn't plan to enter the race this year. Everyone knows that."

"So what are you doing here at Rick's house?" Maria asked.

"Same thing as Julie," Dan said. "I stopped to wish Rick good luck in the race. I may be a poor sledder,

CODY SMITH AND THE HOLIDAY MYSTERIES

but I'm not a poor loser. Rick has a good sled. And he knows how to race it. He deserves to win."

Cody thought about the kids' stories carefully. Maria considered their motives. The two left the other kids for a few moments. And they talked together softly. At last they joined the group again.

"We think we know who took the sled," Cody said.

HOW DID CODY AND MARIA FIGURE OUT WHO TOOK THE SLED?

What was the guilty person's motive?

Find the answer on page 67.

2

The Case of the
Vanished Valentine Box

A Valentine's Day Mystery

Cody stopped in the hallway of Chisholm Trail Middle School. Maria stood right behind him. They listened. They heard Miss Vincent's angry voice. It came from her classroom. Their art teacher sounded near tears.

"I'm determined to find that box!" Miss Vincent yelled.

"Wonder what's up," Cody said. "Miss Vincent is one of my favorite teachers. She hardly ever raises her voice. Let's find out what's going on."

"It's none of our business," Maria said.

"Everything is a detective's business," Cody said. "Come on. Let's see what's going on."

Cody and Maria stepped into the classroom. Three students stood near Miss Vincent's desk.

"Cody! Maria!" Miss Vincent called to them. "I'm glad to see you two. You've solved mysteries before. Maybe you can help me."

Cody and Maria stepped closer to listen. Cody also observed the other students. Good detectives did lots of observing.

"Our valentine box has disappeared," Miss Vincent said. "I had my art students design a valentine box as an art project. I told them they could use it to exchange valentines with their friends. We planned to open it tomorrow—Valentine's Day. Now our plans have been spoiled."

"When did the box disappear?" Maria asked.

"How long has it been missing?" Cody asked.

Miss Vincent sighed. "I'm not really sure. I know it was here this morning. And it was here when I went to lunch. I keep trying to remember the last time I saw it."

"What did the box look like?" Cody asked.

"It was a papier-mâché box," Miss Vincent replied. "The students wrapped it in yards of red crepe paper. Then they glued on pink hearts and cupids. I was very pleased with their artwork."

"Were there lots of valentines in the box?" Maria asked. "Was it heavy? Would it have been hard to carry?"

"It was almost full," Miss Vincent said. "But it didn't weigh very much. And now it's gone. And the valentines are gone."

"What do you think happened to the box?" Cody asked. He looked at the three students standing nearby. Nick, Sarah, and Emily were all acting very nervous.

Nick tugged at the string on his black hooded sweatshirt.

Sarah kept running her fingers through her wet hair. Then she'd wipe her hands on her red-stained shirt.

Emily tugged at the cuff of her boot even though it seemed to be firmly in place.

"I think one of these students took the box," Miss Vincent said. "I remember more clearly now. The box was here a few minutes ago. Then I had to leave the room. The principal called me to his office. The box was here when I left. It was gone when I returned."

"How about it, Nick?" Maria asked. "Have you seen the valentine box? Maybe you don't like the idea of a valentine exchange. Do you think you're too old for valentines?"

"No," Nick admitted. "I put a valentine for Sarah in the box. And I hope she left one for me. I just stopped here today to pick up an art book. I didn't see the box. And I didn't take it either."

"Sarah," Cody said. "Kids say you got the most valentines last year."

"That's right," Sarah said. "But what difference does that make?"

"Were you afraid someone else might get more this year?" Maria asked. "Did you hide the box for that reason?"

"That's not true," Sarah said. Again she ran her fingers through her long, wet hair. "I took a shower after gym class. I started home. But my hair was still wet. So I came back to get my hat. Mom gets mad when I go outside with wet hair."

"Did you see the valentine box when you returned?" Cody asked.

"No," Sarah said. "I didn't see it."

"Emily?" Cody asked. "Did you take the valentine box?"

"No." Emily held up a valentine. "I wanted to put another valentine in the box. It's for a special friend. I didn't want anyone to see me. I looked everywhere. But I couldn't find the box."

"It's a real puzzle," Miss Vincent said. "These are all good students. They're never in trouble. Why would one of them take the valentine box?"

"The 'why' of a case is always interesting," Cody said. "It's usually more important than the 'how' or the 'when.' We need to figure out the 'why' of it."

"Cody and I need to talk privately," Maria said.

"Go ahead," Miss Vincent said. "We'll wait right here."

Cody and Maria stepped into the hallway. They talked quietly for a few moments. Then they returned to the art room.

Cody spoke. "We think we know who took the valentine box."

HOW DID CODY AND MARIA KNOW WHO TOOK THE VALENTINE BOX?

What was the guilty person's motive?

Find the answer on page 68.

3

The Case of the Gaping Gate

A St. Patrick's Day Mystery

Cody and Maria had been cooped up all winter. Today the sun shone and the air felt warm for March.

They decided to go for a brisk walk. They walked to Dillon Road. It was easy to see Blarney House from the road.

The Case of the Gaping Gate

Blarney House belonged to Mrs. McNamara. She had painted it bright green. She was Irish. She said green reminded her of Ireland.

"Cody! Maria!" Mrs. McNamara called to them. "Come quickly. I've heard that you two are detectives. People have told me about the mysteries you've solved. Now I need your help. Someone left my chicken-pen gate open. I want to know who did it."

Cody liked to notice things. Right now he noticed that Mrs. McNamara's shoes were covered with mud.

And he noticed her front porch. Two baseball gloves lay on it. He didn't think Mrs. McNamara played much baseball.

Both Cody and Maria noticed Mrs. McNamara's bulldog, Flannagan.

Flannagan was wearing a green sweater. He was also wearing green stockings. A green hat perched on his head. Flannagan looked unhappy. But then, Cody thought, how could you tell if a bulldog was happy?

"We'll try to help," Cody said. "What's going on? Why is Flannagan dressed in green? And why are there three kids in your front yard?"

Mrs. McNamara sighed. "Troubles seem to come in threes. First, I accidentally left my garden hose on all night. Now the backyard's flooded."

"That's too bad," Cody said.

"Second, Flannagan lost his necklace," Mrs. McNamara said. "It was part of his costume for the

19

St. Patrick's Day parade. He's dressed in green for the parade. I'm sure he lost the necklace in the front yard. That's where he likes to play."

"What's the third thing?" Maria asked.

"Third, someone left the chicken-pen gate open," Mrs. McNamara said. "My special Araucanian hens are running everywhere. They are special chickens from South America. Sometimes they lay green eggs."

Green eggs! Cody almost laughed. But he kept his cool.

One of the chickens flew to Flannagan. It perched on the bulldog's head. Another flew to Mrs. McNamara. It perched on her shoulder. A third chicken perched on the front fender of her car.

"I asked Dave, Nicole, and Carlos to help find Flannagan's necklace," Mrs. McNamara said. "Flannagan's parade costume won't be complete without his necklace. It's made of shamrocks. But so far, nobody has found it. Poor Flannagan!"

"Maybe we should catch the chickens first," Maria said. "We could put them back in the pen."

"Yes," Mrs. McNamara agreed. "That would be a good idea. But I want to know who left that gate open. I think one of these kids did it. Please help me find out which one."

Dave, Nicole, and Carlos were crouched down. They were searching in the grass for Flannagan's necklace. Cody watched them a few moments. Then he spoke.

"Did one of you leave Mrs. McNamara's gate open?"

Nobody answered.

"Dave, did you open the gate?" Cody asked.

"No," Dave said. "I didn't open any gate. Don't try to blame me." Dave stood up and clenched his fists. He looked ready to fight.

"Hey," Cody said. "Let's not fight about this. Fighting doesn't solve problems."

Cody tried to back away. But Dave stepped on his foot. Mud stained the top of Cody's new hiking boot. But Cody held his temper.

"I'm not blaming you, Dave," Cody said. "I'm just trying to figure out the truth. That's what Mrs. McNamara wants."

Dave cooled down. "Here's the truth. Nicole was here when I arrived. We didn't search the backyard. Mrs. McNamara said *front yard.* That's where Flannagan lost his necklace. I didn't go to the backyard. And that's where the chicken pen is."

"What about that, Nicole?" Maria asked. "Is Dave's story true?"

"I suppose so," Nicole said. "I was the first one here. I've only been in the front yard. Dave could have gone to the backyard. I've been looking down at the grass. He could have left without me noticing. But I was never anywhere near the gate."

Cody spoke up again. "Nicole, you were here first. You could have opened the gate. Nobody was around to see you."

"But I didn't open it," Nicole said. "Why would I do that? Why would any of us open the gate? It doesn't make sense."

"You all had a motive of sorts," Maria said. "Mrs. McNamara's green eggs are very special. I've read about Araucanian hens. Maybe you all wanted some green eggs for St. Patrick's Day."

"Maybe so," Mrs. McNamara said. "Maybe so."

"There's a party after the St. Patrick's Day parade," Maria said. "Maybe one of you wanted to take green eggs to the party. So you entered the henhouse and forgot to close the chicken-pen gate."

"Could be," Cody said. "But I don't see anyone with green eggs. What about you, Carlos? Let's hear your story."

"I arrived with Dave," Carlos said. "We were searching for Flannagan's necklace. Dave could have left the front yard. Or Nicole, too, for that matter. But I didn't see them leave. I was looking down at the grass. And I never left the front yard."

"Maybe you kids aren't such good detectives," Mrs. McNamara said. "We still don't know who did it."

"I think I do," Cody said.

"So let's hear it," Mrs. McNamara said.

"I need to talk to Maria first," Cody said. "We're detective partners. We always discuss our cases."

"So go ahead and discuss," Mrs. McNamara said. She grabbed the chicken from her shoulder. She grabbed the chicken from Flannagan's head. And she grabbed the chicken from the car. She put all three chickens back into their pen.

Cody and Maria talked for a few moments. Then they faced the waiting group.

"We think we know who left the gate open," Cody said.

HOW DID CODY AND MARIA KNOW WHO LEFT THE GATE OPEN?

What was the guilty person's motive?

Find the answer on page 69.

4

The Case of the Loose Lid

An Earth Day Mystery

Cody thought about the call from Jeb Logan. Jeb had a mystery for him and Maria. Someone had taken a secret ride on Jeb's stallion—a forbidden ride.

Jeb wanted to know who had done this. He had promised to pick up Cody and Maria at the park. Then they would drive to his ranch and discuss the case.

Right now, Cody carried sunflower seeds and a trowel. Maria carried an empty milk jug. They walked under a stone archway. A sign on it read *COTTONWOOD PARK*.

Cody could barely keep his mind on planting seeds. He wanted to talk to Jeb. But it was Earth Day. He and Maria had some sunflowers to plant.

"Here's the brick flower bed," Cody said. They stopped at a small patch of tilled soil. It lay near a bubbling fountain.

"Mayor Grandwon said we could plant here. He likes these special giant sunflowers." Cody shook the pack of seeds.

"And sunflowers grow well in Kansas," Maria said. "Your mom told me that."

"This is a good way to celebrate Earth Day," Cody said. "The sunflowers will beautify the park all summer. Then the birds can feast on their seeds in the fall."

Cody dug the holes and planted the seeds. Maria dipped her milk jug in the fountain. Then she watered the seeds. She began singing "Home on the Range."

"Why are you singing?" Cody asked.

"Plants grow better when someone talks to them," Maria said. "My mother says so. Surely singing's better than talking. And 'Home on the Range' is the Kansas state song. I think the seeds will like that."

"The plants aren't even up yet," Cody said. "Sometimes you're very strange, Maria. Whoever heard of singing to seeds?"

Maria was about to argue. But a blue pickup truck stopped.

"*BAR-L RANCH*," Cody read the logo on the truck. He recognized rancher Jeb Logan. Everyone in Cottonwood knew Jeb.

"He looks like a real cowboy," Maria whispered. "This is the first time I've seen him up close."

Jeb jumped down from his truck. Cody eyed Jeb's ten-gallon cowboy hat. Jeb was wearing a Western shirt with a bolo tie. His chaps, blue jeans, and cowboy boots completed his outfit. Jeb carried the smell of leather about him.

Jeb Logan *did* look like a real cowboy, Cody thought. Maria was right about some things. But maybe not about singing to sunflower seeds.

"Are you Cody and Maria, the detectives?" Jeb asked.

"Yes," Cody replied. "We've been waiting for you. Do you still have a case for us to solve?"

"Yes," Jeb said. "Can you come to my ranch right now?"

"Sure," Cody said. "My mom said it was okay."

Cody was excited about his visit to the ranch. He helped Maria climb up into the truck.

"I know your mother," Jeb said. "I'll call her on my cell phone. I'll let her know you're with me."

Jeb called Cody's mom. When he finished, Cody spoke.

"We want to help you, Mr. Logan," Cody said. "We want to figure out who rode your stallion."

"Whoever rode Hickok lathered him," Jeb said. "I know that for a fact. She didn't rub Hickok down after the ride."

"Is your horse named after Wild Bill Hickok?" Maria asked.

"Yes," Jeb replied. "Wild Bill was a famous frontier marksman. He spent quite a bit of time in Kansas. It seemed like a good name for my wild stallion.

"But there's something else important you should know," he continued. "Someone left the lid loose on the feed can. That's dangerous business."

"Why is that so dangerous?" Maria asked. "Couldn't you just put the lid back on the can?"

Jeb shook his head. "Horses don't know when to stop eating. They can get sick if they eat too much. I measure Hickok's grain very carefully. Whoever left the loose lid on that grain can needs to learn some ranch manners."

"Maybe this is a job for the police," Cody said. "Tampering with horses is police stuff."

Again Jeb shook his head. "I think riding Hickok was a kid's prank," Jeb said. "I don't want to get anyone in trouble with the police."

"You say '*kid's* prank,'" Maria said. "Are you sure the culprit was a 'kid'?"

"Well, almost," Jeb said. "I hired three kids to help clean stables. I let them pitch a tent in the corral. They slept there all night. They wanted to get an early start this morning. This morning's when I discovered the open feed can. I'm guessing that one of them did it."

The truck arrived at the ranch. Limestone pillars marked the entryway. A white saddle-shaped sign hung on one pillar. Blue letters spelled *LOGAN'S BAR-L RANCH*. Cody could smell newly mowed hay. He liked the Bar-L immediately.

Jeb drove them to the corral. Cody saw the tent. Then he saw the stable. Inside, three kids were forking straw from horse stalls. Jeb called to them. They stopped work and came outside.

"Meet my workers," Jeb said. "This is Amanda, Rachel, and Jenni. I think one of them rode Hickok and left the loose lid on the grain can."

Cody studied the workers. Amanda had one brown eye and one blue eye. That might be important to the case.

Rachel was left-handed. She held her fork in her left hand. Then she dropped it and smoothed her hair with her left hand. That might be important too.

Jenni liked the color red. She wore a red shirt and red pants. Even her socks were red. Could that make a difference to this case? Cody wondered.

"I know these kids from school," Maria said. "They all have motives for taking a secret ride. But not for leaving a loose lid on the grain can. I think that was an accident."

"What motives do they have?" Jeb asked.

"Amanda won a riding trophy last fall," Maria said. "Maybe she rode last night to keep in form. Rachel's a beginning rider. Maybe she just wanted some practice. And Jenni loves to ride anytime. And anyplace. Maybe she went riding just for the fun of it."

Cody smiled. Maria was good at figuring out motives.

"What do all of you have to say for yourselves?" Jeb asked.

"Let's start with you, Amanda," Cody said.

"We were all sleeping in the tent," Amanda said. "I looked up and saw the full moon. The other two cots were empty. But I stayed on my cot all night. I didn't go outside. I didn't do any riding."

Cody thought about Amanda's blue eye and her brown eye. Did they make the world look different? he wondered.

"How about you, Rachel?" Maria asked. "What do you know about this?"

"I got up once to get a drink," Rachel said. "I was sleepy. I didn't notice the other two. I went into the stable to the faucet. But I didn't ride the stallion. And I didn't touch the feed can. I got a drink. Then I came right back to bed."

Did left-handed water taste different? Would it make a girl do strange things? Cody wondered.

"And you, Jenni?" Cody asked. "Did you get up during the night?"

"No," Jenni said. "I slept the whole night through. Amanda couldn't have seen my empty cot. No way. I was in it all night."

Did Jenni have a red sleeping bag? Cody wondered. But what difference would a red sleeping bag make?

"Maria and I need to talk about this privately," Cody said.

Maria followed him to a shade tree. They talked about what they had heard. At last they rejoined the group.

"We know who left the loose lid on the feed can," Cody said.

HOW DID CODY AND MARIA KNOW WHO LEFT THE LOOSE LID?

What was the guilty person's motive?

Find the answer on page 70.

5

The Case of the Jarred Jelly Beans

A May Day Mystery

Maria gathered her art supplies. She had paper, markers, and scissors. She popped a cinnamon ball into her mouth. She was about to clap her radio headphones over her ears.

Suddenly, the telephone rang. Maria answered and heard Tillie Twinkle's voice.

"Are you coming, Maria? Please hurry," Miss Twinkle said. "Something terrible has happened. I need your help."

"I'll be right there, Miss Twinkle," Maria said. "I'm leaving right now."

"What's going on?" Cody asked. "Miss Twinkle's voice was loud. I could almost hear every word."

"I wish you were going with me," Maria said. "But she only invited Amber, Gina, and me. She promised to help us make May baskets."

"But why was she so upset?" Cody asked.

"Miss Twinkle said something terrible has happened," explained Maria.

"I don't really want to make May baskets with the girls anyway," Cody said. "But I do mind missing out on a mystery. This would be a great day for tracking criminals."

"What makes you think so?" Maria asked.

"It rained hard last night," Cody said. "We had six inches of rain in an hour. So there's plenty of mud. This would be a great day for finding footprints."

Maria sighed. Cody was right. This was a good day for following footprints. It was too bad he wasn't coming along to Miss Twinkle's. She wondered what terrible thing had happened.

Tillie Twinkle lived across the street. Maria hurried to her house. Miss Twinkle loved to paint. Her home always smelled like oils and turpentine. Maria liked those artist smells.

She liked Miss Twinkle's pictures too. Miss Twinkle liked to paint dancing ballerinas. Dozens of ballerinas hung on her walls. She had signed them all with her whole name—Tillie Thelma Twinkle.

She said she wanted to paint like Edgar Degas. He was a famous French painter and sculptor. He was known for his paintings of ballet dancers.

But today Miss Twinkle wasn't painting ballerinas. She was wiping her nose. And she was sniffling into her handkerchief.

"Maria!" Miss Twinkle said. "I'm so glad you've arrived. Someone has ruined my day. And I think one of these girls is to blame." Miss Twinkle gestured toward the two girls who were sitting nearby. "Both Gina and Amber are my neighbors. But I think one of them is a thief."

"They're my neighbors too," Maria said. "And they're my friends. Surely neither of them is a thief."

"Wait until you hear my story," Miss Twinkle said. "These girls arrived early. And they were eager to make May baskets. They put their art supplies on the dining room table. There's lots of work space there."

"Go on," Maria said. Miss Twinkle still looked as if she might cry.

"I had a jar of yellow jelly beans," Miss Twinkle said. "They were on my back porch. I planned to give them to you girls. They were for your May baskets. Now the jelly beans are gone. I think Gina or Amber took them. They could see them on the porch."

Maria looked at Gina. Gina didn't look like a thief. But she liked yellow. She wore a yellow shirt, yellow pants, and yellow sandals. She even had a yellow scrunchie in her blond hair. Maybe she liked yellow jelly beans too.

Then Maria looked at Amber. Everyone knew Amber liked to eat. She was plump. She wore a denim jumper and a white T-shirt. She had red hair like Cody's. Freckles dotted her face. She didn't look like a thief either.

But what does a thief look like? Maria wondered. She remembered pictures she had seen on the post office wall. Not one of them wore a yellow hair scrunchie—or a denim jumper.

"Miss Twinkle," Maria said. "Why do you think Amber or Gina is the thief?"

"Both girls made excuses to leave my house," Miss Twinkle said. "And they left through the back porch. Right after they returned, the jar of jelly beans was missing."

"Let's hear what you have to say, girls," Maria said. "Who wants to speak first?"

"I will," Amber said. "My mom had to run an errand. But she was expecting a phone call. Our house is right next door. So she asked me to listen for the phone. She left the windows open so I could hear it."

"Did it ring?" Maria asked.

"Yes, it did," Amber said. "That's why I left Miss Twinkle's house. I ran home to answer the telephone. I took a message for my mother. Then I came right back here. I didn't take the jar of jelly beans."

"What about you, Gina?" Maria asked. "Why did you leave Miss Twinkle's house?"

"I saw a robin in the tree outside," Gina said. "Seeing it reminded me of something. I promised Mom to fill our birdbath every day."

"And that's why you left the house?" Maria asked.

"Yes," Gina said. "I don't get my allowance until I do my chores. Today I was excited about making May baskets. I forgot all about chores. When I remembered, I ran home and filled the birdbath. But I came right back. I didn't take the jelly beans."

"Miss Twinkle, both of their stories sound true," Maria said. "I need to think about this."

"Take your time," Mrs. Twinkle said.

"Both girls have a motive for taking the jelly beans," Maria said.

"Of course," Miss Twinkle said. "That's obvious. Everyone likes to eat jelly beans."

"We all know Amber likes to eat," Maria said. "Maybe she just wanted to eat the jelly beans. And Gina loves yellow. Maybe she wanted yellow jelly beans for her May basket. Maybe she wanted her basket to match her outfit."

"This isn't helping me," Miss Twinkle said.

Maria thought a while longer. She was tempted to call Cody for help. Then she remembered something Cody had said.

"I know who took the jelly beans, " Maria said.

HOW DID MARIA KNOW WHO TOOK THE JELLY BEANS?

What was the guilty person's motive?

Find the answer on page 71.

6

The Case of the Broken Begonias

A Flag Day Mystery

Cody hurried to Mrs. Flowers' house. She expected him to walk her Irish wolfhound, Muldoon. He wanted to be on time. This was his first paying job!

Cody needed money for a fingerprinting kit. All good detectives owned fingerprinting kits.

Mrs. Flowers greeted him at her garden gate. "You won't be able to walk Muldoon today, Cody," she said. "Terrible things have happened. And on Flag Day too. Flag Day is my favorite holiday. And now it's ruined."

"What bad things have happened?" Cody asked. He looked around. He didn't see Muldoon.

But he saw Mrs. Flowers' begonia plants. Someone had stepped on them. The plants were broken.

"First, Muldoon's in trouble," Mrs. Flowers said. "He ran off yesterday morning. And he trampled Mrs. Leeds' petunias. I had to send him to obedience school. He'll be away for a week. I miss him already."

"I'll miss him too," Cody said. "I wanted to walk him for you. I like all dogs. But I especially like Muldoon. He's big and friendly. And he always smells good."

Cody didn't add that he needed the money. Employers knew about a kid's need for money, didn't they?

"You'll get to walk Muldoon next week," Mrs. Flowers promised. "But something else bad has happened. Someone crushed my begonia plants. I needed them for the Flag Day parade. I'm a patriotic gardener. I raise red roses, white begonias, and lovely bluebells."

"They're all very pretty," Cody said. "Except the ruined begonias, of course. They don't look so good right now."

"Please help me find who did this," Mrs. Flowers said.

"Tell me more about it," Cody said. "Do you have any clues? Tell me all the details."

"I promised to provide a patriotic display," Mrs. Flowers said. "It was for the judge's platform at the Flag Day parade. But now I have no white flowers. I must find out who ruined them."

"I'll try to help," Cody said. "Do you have any idea who would do this? Everyone likes you and Muldoon. I don't know why anyone would ruin your begonias."

"I hired three children to help me garden. Adam, Marta, and Ryan were supposed to water the begonias this morning. I think one of them did this."

"Where are they now?" Cody asked.

"They're waiting on my back porch," Mrs. Flowers said. "Will you talk to them?"

Cody and Mrs. Flowers walked to the back porch. Cody saw his friends waiting there. Marta held a watering can. She looked sad.

Adam held the watering hose. He looked sad too.

But Ryan just looked angry. His rusty bicycle lay near the begonias.

"This is going to be a tough case," Cody said. "Each of you has a motive for blaming the others."

"How do you know that?" Mrs. Flowers asked.

"They look like ordinary kids to me. What sort of motives do they have?"

"These kids are my friends," Cody said. "I understand them. They don't want to lose their gardening jobs here. That's one strong motive."

"That may be true," Mrs. Flowers agreed. "I pay a good wage for good work. But I don't pay for ruined begonias."

"I know how these kids feel," Cody said. "I don't want to lose my job walking Muldoon. We're all saving money for special projects."

"Right," Adam said. And they all nodded.

"I'm saving for a fingerprint kit," Cody said. "Ryan's saving for a new bike. Adam's saving for a video game. And Marta's saving for new software. Right?"

They all nodded.

"I'll let you talk to them alone," Mrs. Flowers said. "You understand them better than I do. Just find out who ruined my begonias. I want to talk to that person." Mrs. Flowers flounced into the house.

"Do you know who broke the begonias?" Cody asked. He looked at them one at a time. Nobody answered him. "I don't want to get anyone in trouble. If you broke the begonias, just admit it. Telling the truth usually helps make things right."

Nobody spoke.

"How about you, Marta. Can you tell us what happened?"

"No," Marta said. "I arrived here first this morning. The begonias were okay then. And I didn't break them. Then Ryan got here. The begonias were still okay then. Right, Ryan?"

"That's right," Ryan said.

"But I had to leave for a few minutes," Marta said. "When I returned, Ryan was still here. Adam was just arriving. And the begonias were broken."

"What do you say, Adam?" Cody asked.

"Nothing," Adam said. "Marta's telling the truth. The begonias were broken when I arrived."

"Well, I have plenty to say," Ryan said. "You're making it sound as if I did this. But that's not true. Marta left for a while. Adam hadn't arrived yet. While I was here alone, I saw Muldoon run through the begonias."

"Are you sure?" Cody asked.

"Of course I'm sure," Ryan said. "Muldoon trampled them. He has huge feet. He sat on some of them. Then he rolled right in the center of the bed. Muldoon's the culprit. None of us is guilty. Her own dog's to blame."

"That could be true," Marta added. "Mrs. Leeds says that Muldoon ruined her petunias."

Cody wished Maria were here. Two heads were better than one. He walked to the begonia bed. He sat beside Ryan's bicycle to think.

At last he walked to Mrs. Flowers' door.

"Mrs. Flowers," he called. "I know who broke your begonias."

HOW DID CODY KNOW WHO BROKE THE BEGONIAS?

What was the guilty person's motive?

Find the answer on page 72.

7

The Case of the Early Ears

An Independence Day Mystery

Cody raced to the telephone on the first ring. He and Maria had a rule—NEVER LET A PHONE RING TWICE.

But they played fair. Whoever answered the phone pushed the speaker button. Then both of them could listen to the conversation.

"This is Mrs. Husker," the voice said. "I would like to speak to Detective Cody Smith."

Cody almost dropped the telephone in surprise. He seldom received telephone requests for his services. Maria stepped closer to the telephone.

"This is Cody Smith," he replied.

"I have a case for you," Mrs. Husker said. "It involves some of your friends. That's why I've called you. Can you come to my house? I live on Old Jayhawk Road."

"I'll be right over," Cody said. "I'll bring my partner Maria. What is this case about?"

"I'll tell you when you get here," Mrs. Husker said and hung up.

"Let's go, Cody," Maria said.

It was the Fourth of July. Cody and Maria had plans to celebrate. But the celebration would have to wait. A mystery to solve was more important.

They walked the short distance to Mrs. Husker's house. Cody jingled coins in his pocket. Maria jingled coins too. She carried half of their money. They planned to solve a mystery. But they also planned to buy sweet corn for their holiday dinner.

"Do you think Mrs. Husker's corn will be ready?" Maria asked. "It's very early. *Corn knee-high by the Fourth of July.* That's a popular saying in Kansas."

"But Mrs. Husker's corn is different," Cody said. "Mom says Mrs. Husker raises Early Ear sweet corn. It's ready to eat before other kinds. Mrs. Husker is very popular with corn lovers on Independence Day."

They stepped into Mrs. Husker's yard. Mrs. Husker stood on her porch. She was talking on a cordless telephone. Actually, Cody noticed, she was just listening.

The telephone caller shouted at her. She held the receiver away from her ear. Cody could hear the angry words.

People were also shouting at her as they drove by her house. Today Mrs. Husker was not popular at all—at least not with people.

Today Mrs. Husker was only popular with mosquitoes. She put down her phone and adjusted her straw hat. Mosquito netting hung from the hat's brim. She carried a fly swatter in her hand.

The mosquitoes buzzed around her head. She swatted at them with the fly swatter.

She missed.

She swatted again.

And all the time, her telephone kept ringing. And all the time, people drove by to shout at her.

"Oh, children!" Mrs. Husker cried. "I'm so glad you're here. I need your help."

Cody pulled himself to his full height. He liked it when adults needed his help.

Maria just smiled. She was thinking about the story she might write about this mystery. Each new case gave her more story material.

"Tell us about your mystery," Cody said. "But shouldn't you answer your telephone first? Someone might be calling to buy sweet corn."

"I'm going to turn that phone off," Mrs. Husker said. "People aren't calling to buy my sweet corn. They're calling to complain about the mosquitoes. I'm on the Cottonwood City Council. People keep calling to tell me that the city should spray for mosquitoes."

"That might be a good idea," Maria said. She watched Mrs. Husker swat at a mosquito. Another one bit the end of her nose.

"The city doesn't have any money for mosquito spray," Mrs. Husker said.

"Then tell us about your mystery," Maria said. "The mosquitoes aren't biting us. We dab vanilla extract behind our ears. Cody's mom had that idea. She says mosquitoes don't like vanilla extract."

Mrs. Husker looked surprised. Then she pointed to the three children standing near her corn patch.

"I set a dozen ears of sweet corn on my porch," Mrs. Husker said. "I put them in a basket. They were for a customer. Now they're missing. I hired Ali, Luis, and Megan. They were going to help me pick corn today. But I think one of them took my basket of sweet corn."

"Which one of them?" Maria asked.

"I don't know," Mrs. Husker said. "That's my problem."

Cody and Maria stepped closer to the kids. Cody tried not to laugh. Ali was wearing long pants. A long-sleeved sweater covered her arms. A stocking cap covered her ears. And a scarf covered her neck. She fanned herself with a corn leaf.

"Why all the clothes?" Cody asked.

"I'm trying to keep the mosquitoes off," Ali said. "And don't blame the missing corn on me. I was last to arrive here. I didn't see any corn on the porch."

Maria stepped closer to Luis. Then she backed away. "What's that smell, Luis?" she asked. "It smells just a little bit like . . . skunk."

"It's mosquito repellent," Luis said. "My grandpa makes it. It's an old family recipe. It works for him. And it works for me too. It keeps the mosquitoes away."

"I can understand why," Cody said. "I'm guessing it repels more than mosquitoes." He held his hand over his nose. "Did you see the corn on Mrs. Husker's porch, Luis?"

"I'm no corn thief," Luis said. "I arrived here first. The corn was on the porch then. It was in a peck basket. But I didn't take it. I walked into the corn patch and began picking. I've been there ever since I arrived. Don't blame the theft on me."

Cody looked at Megan. She wore a jumpsuit. It was red, white, and blue. Only a few mosquitoes buzzed around her. Maybe the mosquitoes felt patriotic today.

"What about you, Megan?" Cody asked. "What do you know about the missing corn?"

"I was second to arrive," Megan said. "And the corn was on the porch. I didn't take it. I just picked up an empty basket. Then I walked into the patch to work."

"So Luis saw the corn on the porch," Cody said. "And Megan saw it too. But Ali arrived last. And she didn't see it."

"Don't try to blame me," Megan said. "I live right next door. Mom's having a patio party this evening. I promised her I'd sweep the patio. But I forgot. When I remembered, I ran home. I swept the patio and came back. Someone could have taken the corn while I was gone."

"All of you have a motive for taking the corn," Maria said. "You would all like sweet corn for your Fourth of July dinner. One of you probably took it for your family."

"Maria is good at figuring out motives," Cody said. "Now we need to discuss your motives and clues privately. Please stay right where you are."

Cody motioned Maria to the porch. They talked. They reviewed what each person had said. At last they returned to Mrs. Husker.

"We know who took your Early Ears," Cody said.

HOW DID CODY AND MARIA KNOW WHO
TOOK THE EARLY EARS?

What was the guilty person's motive?

Find the answer on page 73.

8

The Case of the Creamed Costumes

A Labor Day Mystery

Cody Smith tried on his Sherlock Holmes hat. It fit perfectly. So did Maria's. Maria's parents were still working in Italy. Sometimes they sent gifts to Cody and her.

Maria would rather have her parents than gifts. But that was life. And she liked the detective hats. So did Cody.

"Hurry up, Maria," Cody yelled. "We don't want to miss any of the Labor Day parade. It's going to start soon. And it will be a long one. The judge's reviewing stand is almost a mile away."

"I can hear a band," Maria said.

"That's because you're wearing your radio headphones," Cody said. "The parade band isn't playing yet."

"Oh," Maria said. She took off the headphones carefully. Wearing both headphones and a Sherlock Holmes hat wasn't easy.

Ms. Wanda Workman called to them from her yard. They went to see what she wanted. Cody looked at her red face. He saw her stamp her foot and scowl.

"Kids," she muttered, "I need help. Mrs. Flowers told me that you solved her broken-begonia case. Maybe you can figure out this mystery."

"Tell us about it," Cody said, smiling. He was happy to hear that Mrs. Flowers had praised his and Maria's detective skills.

"Someone sprayed whipped cream on my burglar costumes," Ms. Workman said. "Three girls were supposed to wear the costumes. But I think one of them did this. Please come take a look. I want to find the guilty person."

Cody and Maria followed Ms. Workman to her parade float. It was parked at the curb.

Cody read the big sign on the float. "Workman Security Systems."

Maria read a smaller sign. "For Sure-Locked Homes, Call Wanda Workman."

"A clever play on words," Cody said.

"Thank you," Ms. Workman said. "I've worked hard. I've made a success of my security-alarm business. And that's what this Labor Day parade is all about. It honors workers."

Ms. Workman motioned to them to follow her. They followed her to the backyard. Cody saw three of his friends sitting on the back porch. Amy, Christy, and Diana looked like unhappy campers. Or, Cody thought, unhappy burglars.

The costumes hung on the clothesline. Streaks of white whipped cream clung to the shirts. Whipped cream drooled from the pockets of the jeans. Now the black stocking caps had white topknots.

"Did one of you spray whipped cream on the costumes?" Cody asked.

The girls didn't answer. They stared straight ahead.

"See," Ms. Workman said. "They won't even talk."

"Maybe they don't like the costumes," Maria said. "Black turtleneck shirts. Black jeans. Black masks.

Black stocking caps. Black gloves. They aren't very exciting. Maybe that's why they sprayed the whipped cream."

Cody admired Maria for figuring out motives. But today he had one of his own.

"It's a hot day," Cody said. "You would roast in those costumes on a hot day."

"But I always use these costumes," Ms. Workman said. "I've saved them from year to year. This year they smelled musty. So I hung them on the clothesline. They needed fresh air and sunshine. But now look at them."

Cody studied the girls carefully. White specks dotted Amy's red T-shirt. A white patch stained Christy's blue shorts. Diana's right wrist looked white and sticky.

Honeybees began swarming around the costumes. Then they buzzed around the three girls.

"What do you have to say, Christy?" Cody asked. "Did you spray the costumes?"

"Don't blame me," Christy said. "I arrived first. The costumes were okay when I got here. Then I ran across the street for a few minutes. I wanted to see the float from White's Laundromat. When I returned, the costumes had been sprayed."

"And you, Amy?" Maria asked. "What do you know about these spoiled costumes?" Maria brushed at a honeybee flying around her head.

"I didn't see who did it," Amy said. "I had to take a soda to my Aunt Minnie. She's at the reviewing stand. I wasn't gone over five minutes. The costumes were okay when I left. Christy and Diana were here when I got back. The costumes were a mess then."

"Don't blame me," Diana said. "The costumes were okay when I arrived. Then I went home for a cool drink. Christy and Amy were here when I returned. And the costumes . . . well, you can see for yourself." She giggled. "But the bees like them."

"Maria and I need to talk about this privately," Cody said. "This is a real mystery." They stepped aside and spoke in whispers.

"We think we know who sprayed whipped cream on the costumes," Cody reported.

HOW DID CODY AND MARIA FIGURE OUT WHO CREAMED THE COSTUMES?
What was the guilty person's motive?

Find the answer on page 74.

9

The Case of the Purloined Pie

A Thanksgiving Mystery

Thanksgiving Day! Cody looked outside at the falling snow. He listened to sounds from the kitchen. Dishes clinked against silverware. Pans rattled. His mother was preparing a holiday dinner.

Cody smelled the roasting turkey. He breathed in sage dressing. And best of all, the scent of pumpkin pie floated through the air.

Cody's mom had told him that he had many things to be thankful for this year. Right now, Cody felt very thankful for their Thanksgiving dinner.

"Cody," his mom called from the kitchen. "Mrs. Widen just telephoned me. Someone has stolen one of her Thanksgiving pies."

"Who would do that?" Cody asked.

"It's a mystery," his mom said. "Mrs. Widen wants you and Maria to come to her house. She thinks you can help find the pie thief."

"Hey, Maria," Cody called. "Great news! We have a mystery to solve. Let's go find out more about it."

"Okay," Maria said. She popped a cinnamon ball into her mouth. She offered Cody one too. "I heard that Maya, Tomas, and Jason promised to help Mrs. Widen. They were going to deliver her pies to shut-ins."

"I saw them walking toward her house a while ago," Cody said.

"Then let's go," Maria said. "Let's find out what's happened. Aren't you happy that Mrs. Widen called us?"

"You know it!" Cody replied. It was another thing to be thankful for.

The Case of the Purloined Pie

Cody and Maria ran down the street to Mrs. Widen's house. She met them at the door. She stood only a bit taller than Cody. She almost filled the doorway. And her hair was the color of flour.

The fragrance of nutmeg surrounded Mrs. Widen. Cody wondered if she wore nutmeg instead of perfume.

He heard voices talking in the kitchen. It sounded like his friends. He hoped they weren't in trouble.

"Come on in, kids," Mrs. Widen said. "I'm glad to see you. I need your help. I had three pumpkin pies to deliver. They're special pies for dear friends. They're shut-ins who can't go out for Thanksgiving dinner. And they aren't expecting the pies. The surprise makes it all the more fun."

"You're very kind to make so many pies," Maria said.

"Cooking's my favorite thing," Mrs. Widen said. "I'm happiest in my kitchen." Then she frowned. "But right now I'm very angry. One of my pies is missing. Come with me to the kitchen."

They followed her into the warm, steamy kitchen.

"I had the three pies right here on my kitchen table," Mrs. Widen said. "I packed each pie in its own box. I tied each box with a shiny brown ribbon. And I placed a name and address on each box."

"There are only two boxes here now," Cody said. "Pies just can't disappear on their own."

"Tell us more," Maria said. "Did you leave the pies alone? Did you leave your house?"

"Well, yes, I did," Mrs. Widen said. "These children were about to pick up their pies. Then the telephone rang. A neighbor called. She asked me to help her with her turkey. She needed help lifting it into her oven."

"So you ran next door to help her," Cody guessed.

"Right," Mrs. Widen said. "I told these children to wait. I wanted to give them last minute instructions. I returned in less than ten minutes."

"Then what happened?" Cody asked.

"I saw that one pie was missing," Mrs. Widen said. "It was on the table when I left home. It was gone when I came back. These three children must know something about this. I think one of them took it."

"But which one?" Cody asked. "That's the problem." He looked at his three friends. He didn't want to get anyone in trouble.

"You and Maria have solved several mysteries in this neighborhood," Mrs. Widen said. "What do you say about this one? Can you figure it out for me?"

"We'll try," Cody said. He turned to the three sitting at the table. "Did one of you take Mrs. Widen's pie?"

At first, nobody answered. Then all three of them shouted, "NO!"

"One at a time, please," Maria said. "How about you, Maya? Do you know what happened to the pie?"

"No," Maya said. "I ran home to get my mittens. The pies were here when I left. So were Tomas and Jason. When I returned, one pie was gone. I don't know what happened to it. But Tomas and Jason were in the kitchen with it when I left."

"What about you, Jason?" Cody asked. "Can you tell us what happened to the pie?"

"No," Jason said. "After Maya left, I noticed my dog, Bowser, in Mrs. Widen's backyard."

"How'd he get there?" Maria asked.

"He leaped over the fence," Jason explained. "We live next door."

"Leaped?" Cody asked. "How could he do that? Her fence is very high."

"Sometimes Bowser gets excited when it snows. Then he jumps the fence," Jason said. "I dashed outside to take him back home."

"Then what happened?" Maria asked. "Did you see Maya or Tomas outside? And what about Mrs. Widen? Did you see her outside?"

"I didn't see anyone outside," Jason said. "It took me a long time to catch Bowser and take him home. When I returned to the kitchen, Tomas was here. So was Maya. But the pumpkin pie was gone."

"What about you, Tomas?" Cody asked. "You

were alone in the kitchen when Jason left. You had a perfect opportunity to take the pie."

"No, I didn't," Tomas said. "Right after Jason left, I heard the mail truck outside. Its tires were spinning in the snow. So I went outside to bring in Mrs. Widen's mail. When I returned, Maya was back and the pie was gone."

"What do you make of all this, detectives?" Mrs. Widen asked. "Who do you think took the pie?"

Cody and Maria stepped into the living room to talk.

"They all have good alibis," Maria said. "Maybe Mrs. Widen took her own pie."

"Get real, Maria," Cody said. "Why would she do that? That doesn't make any sense at all."

"You're right," Maria said. "Mrs. Widen wouldn't have taken her own pie."

"I think I know who did it," Cody said at last. He whispered to Maria.

Maria thought for a moment. Then she nodded. "Yes," she agreed. "You're right."

Cody and Maria returned to the kitchen.

"We know who took your pumpkin pie," Cody said.

HOW DID CODY AND MARIA KNOW WHO TOOK THE PIE?

What was the guilty person's motive?

Find the answer on page 75.

10

The Case of the
Cherry Chocolate

A Christmas Mystery

Cody hurried to Mrs. Noel's house. She had called him and Maria. She had a mystery for them to solve. She said something about a carpet—and candy. She had talked so fast they couldn't understand her.

Now he and Maria rushed to Mrs. Noel's house. They wanted to learn more about the mystery.

Cody heard the house before he reached it. Maria heard the Noel house too. Sound poured from it. Even the closed windows didn't stop the sound.

"Why is it so loud?" Cody asked.

"Mr. Noel is hearing impaired," Maria said. "Your mother told me that Mr. Noel keeps the television volume tuned to LOUD. Everyone in the neighborhood can hear the Noel house. And it's worse in the summertime."

"I get tired of the noise," Mrs. Wise said. She lived north of the Noels. She was outside shoveling snow. She had overheard Cody and Maria talking.

"I just close my doors and windows," Ms. Bethlehem said. She waved to Cody and Maria. She lived south of the Noels.

It had snowed last night. Several of the neighbors were outside shoveling.

"I just turn my hearing aid off," Miss LeToe said. "I don't hear a thing." She lived across the street from the Noels.

Cody could smell Mrs. Noel's house too. The scents of holiday baking filled the cold, crisp air. Cody took three deep breaths.

Mrs. Noel had a candy shop in her home. The fragrance of chocolate sweetened the whole neighborhood.

"It smells wonderful," Maria said.

"Sometimes I just stand outside and breathe," Mrs. Bethlehem said. "The good smell makes up for the loud TV."

"I think so too," Mrs. Wise agreed. "I smell cherry-chocolate fudge. Maybe I'll buy some today. Christmas is candy time."

Miss LeToe didn't say anything. She had turned her hearing aid off. But Cody saw her taking deep breaths.

Mrs. Noel greeted them at the door. She reminded Cody of an elf. Their eyes met on the same level. She was short and pencil slim. And her hair stood up in silvery wisps. Usually, Mrs. Noel looked jolly. But today she looked unhappy.

"Cody! Maria!" she cried out. "Please come in. I need your help to solve this mystery."

"What's happened?" Cody asked. The TV *was* really loud. He could hardly hear her. But he heard his favorite word—*mystery*.

"We'll help if we can," Maria said. "Tell us about it."

"I made a pan of cherry-chocolate fudge," Mrs. Noel shouted. "I started to pour it into molds. Then my husband called me. I left the kitchen for just a few minutes."

"Are you sure about that?" Maria asked. "Time flies when you're having chocolate."

"I'm sure I wasn't gone over five minutes," Mrs. Noel said. "When I returned, someone had spilled the cherry chocolate. It lay puddled on the kitchen carpet."

"How could that be?" Maria asked.

"I hired three neighborhood kids to help me today," Mrs. Noel said. "I had some rush orders for Christmas. It's my favorite holiday."

"Really?" Cody asked. He tried to act interested in Mrs. Noel's favorite holiday. But he was really interested in the mystery—and the cherry-chocolate fudge. It smelled delicious—even on the floor.

"I hired Ling, Mark, and Lisa to wrap packages," Mrs. Noel said. "I think one of them spilled the chocolate. Just come look at the mess. What am I going to do? My customers will be so disappointed."

Cody and Maria stepped into the kitchen. The chocolate pan lay tipped on its side. Cherry-chocolate fudge dripped from the stove to the carpet.

Ling had chocolate on her left hand.

Mark had chocolate on his right hand.

And Lisa had chocolate on her chin.

"They had no business in my kitchen!" Mrs. Noel accused. "They were supposed to wrap packages in the front room. I want to know who's guilty. I'll never hire that person again."

"What do all of you have to say?" Cody asked the kids. He knew all three from school. So did Maria.

Ling had dark hair like Maria's. She got top grades in math.

Mark liked to write like Maria. He was the editor of the school paper.

And Lisa was athletic. Her favorite sport was basketball.

"Well, what do you have to say about this spilled candy?" Cody asked again.

Nobody answered Cody's question. So he tried another time.

"Ling, what do you know about the spilled chocolate?"

"Don't blame it on me," Ling said. "I was wrapping packages out front. Then I heard Mark and Lisa talking. They were in the kitchen. When I got here, I saw this mess. But I wasn't around when it happened."

"How about you, Mark?" Maria asked. "What do you know about this?"

"I was wrapping packages out front," Mark said. "Then I heard the kitchen faucet dripping. I came out to turn it off. The chocolate was already on the floor."

"And you, Lisa?" Cody asked.

"I came to the kitchen to check on Mark," Lisa said. "The chocolate was already spilled. But Mark wasn't standing near it. I think Mrs. Noel spilled it herself. I think she's just trying to blame us."

"All of you had a motive for spilling the chocolate," Maria said.

"Motive!" Ms. Noel exclaimed. "I don't believe it. Who would ruin my candy on purpose?"

"Maybe they really didn't want to work," Maria said. "There's a basketball game at school in half an hour. Maybe they wanted to go. If the chocolate spilled, there'd be no candy to wrap. And all of them could go to the game."

"I think I know who did this," Cody said. "Maria, let's talk this over."

Cody and Maria stepped into the front room. They discussed the case. Cody didn't think anyone did it on purpose. Finally, Maria agreed with him. Then they returned to the kitchen.

"We know who spilled the chocolate," Maria said.

HOW DID CODY AND MARIA KNOW WHO SPILLED THE CHOCOLATE?

What was the guilty person's motive?
Find the answer on page 76.

Solutions

MYSTERY #1

The Case of the Slippery Sled

"We think Julie's guilty because she fibbed," Cody said. "The Mouthketeers made a vow to avoid sticky treats. So Julie wouldn't have gone inside for bubble gum. Gum might stick to her braces."

"I don't think Julie would break the vow," Maria said. "So she must have taken the sled. There was no one around when she got here. She had a perfect opportunity to take the sled."

Julie blushed. "I've never owned a sled. I don't know why I thought I could get away with taking Rick's. I'm sorry."

"It's okay, Julie," Rick said. "I have another sled you can borrow. We can both join the race."

MYSTERY #2

The Case of the Vanished Valentine Box

"We think Sarah's guilty," Cody said. "We noticed Sarah's wet hands. And the red stains on her shirt."

"Everyone knows that wet crepe paper fades," Maria said. "Sarah must have held the box. The red crepe paper faded on to her wet hands. Then she wiped her hands on her shirt."

"Right, Sarah?" Maria asked.

"I was going to put it back," answered Sarah. "All I wanted to do was put in a valentine for Scott, the new boy. I was afraid that other kids would make fun of me if they knew I liked him. So I sneaked in here to put my valentine in the box. Then I heard Miss Vincent returning. I panicked and grabbed the box. It's hidden in the closet. I meant to put it back as soon as the room was empty again."

"Well," Miss Vincent said, "no harm has been done. Bring the box back and we'll forget all about it."

"Thanks, Miss Vincent," Sarah said and turned to get the box.

"And, Sarah," Miss Vincent added. "Don't forget the valentine for Scott."

MYSTERY #3

The Case of the Gaping Gate

"We think Dave left the gate open," Cody said. "Mrs. McNamara left her hose running all night. Water flooded the backyard. She has mud on her shoes from walking in the backyard. Dave also has muddy shoes."

"Everyone else has dry shoes," Maria said. "So Dave must have been in the backyard. He must be the guilty one."

"Okay," Dave said. "So I left the gate open. I'm sorry. But I wasn't stealing eggs."

"I accidentally tossed my baseball over the fence," Dave said. "I went inside the chicken pen to get it. And I forgot to close the gate. I'm really sorry, Mrs. McNamara."

"All the chickens are back," Mrs. McNamara said. "And no eggs are missing. So I suppose we can just forget about it."

"Let's all go enjoy the St. Patrick's Day parade," Cody said. "I see Flannagan's necklace right now."

Cody pulled the necklace from under Flannagan's green sweater. It wasn't lost after all.

MYSTERY #4

The Case of the Loose Lid

"We think Amanda is the culprit," Cody said. "She said she looked up and saw the full moon. That's impossible. She was inside the tent. She would only see the tent canvas. The full moon was outside."

"What do you say, Amanda?" Jeb asked.

"Cody's right," Amanda admitted. "I rode your horse. I won't do it again. The loose lid was an accident. I must have bumped it. After this, I'll be more careful around feed cans. I'm sorry I caused trouble. But I was afraid to confess. I didn't want to lose my job."

"It's all right this time," Jeb said. "And you can keep your job. You're a hard worker and a good rider. Maybe you can even teach the others to ride. But you must remember to cool the horses down after you ride them. And be careful around the feed cans."

"I will," Amanda said.

"Maybe you can teach Maria and me to ride," Cody said.

"You can come and ride at my ranch anytime," Jeb said. "As thanks for solving this mystery."

MYSTERY #5

The Case of the Jarred Jelly Beans

"I think Gina took the jelly bean jar," Maria said. "She fibbed about filling the birdbath. It rained hard last night. Rainwater would have filled the birdbath. So Gina had no reason to go home. Right, Gina?"

"I only took them as a joke," Gina said. "I intended to bring them back. I have a bag of green jelly beans at home. I planned to mix them with the yellow ones. Then our May baskets would be green and yellow."

"But why didn't you bring the jar of mixed jelly beans back?" Maria asked.

"I did. It's in my supply bag. When I got back, Miss Twinkle was on the back porch. I couldn't put it back then. I was waiting for a chance to do it when no one was looking. Then you came over and I never had a chance to put it back."

"Can we see it?" Miss Twinkle asked.

"Sure," Gina replied. She pulled the jar from her bag. Sure enough, the jar was filled with yellow *and* green jelly beans.

"I'm sorry my joke turned out so badly," Gina apologized.

"We forgive you, Gina," Maria said. "After all, we'll have the most colorful May baskets in the neighborhood."

MYSTERY #6

The Case of the Broken Begonias

"I think Ryan broke the begonias," Cody said. "He fibbed to us. Ryan couldn't have seen Muldoon ruin the flowers. Muldoon is at obedience school. How about it, Ryan?"

Ryan's face flushed. "You're right," he said. "The brakes on my bike failed. I rode through the begonias before I could stop. I'm really sorry, Mrs. Flowers. I'm sorry for ruining your begonias. And I'm sorry for not admitting I did it. But I was afraid I'd lose my job."

"I won't say it's all right, Ryan," Mrs. Flowers said. "But I accept your apology. And I'll give you a second chance. Tomorrow you can help replant the begonia bed."

"We'll all help," Cody said. "And this time, we'll work for free."

MYSTERY #7

The Case of the Early Ears

"We think Megan took the corn," Cody said. "I think she fibbed about her mother having a patio party. Nobody would plan an outdoor party today. The mosquitoes are too bad."

"What about it, Megan?" Mrs. Husker asked.

Megan looked at her toes. "Yes, I took it. I thought it would be something special for our Fourth of July cookout. I'm sorry. I'll bring it back."

"I need that corn today. But I'll save you some next week," Mrs. Husker said. "You can pay for it by working for me."

Mrs. Husker turned to Cody and Maria. "I'll save you some extra special ears too."

Cody and Maria couldn't wait.

MYSTERY #8

The Case of the Creamed Costumes

"We think Amy creamed the costumes," Cody said. "She fibbed about going to the reviewing stand. The stand is almost a mile away. There's no way she could have gone there and back in five minutes."

"Okay, you're right," Amy said. "But I'm not taking the blame all by myself. We all creamed the costumes. We're tired of wearing them. They're too hot. We tried to tell Ms. Workman. But she wouldn't listen."

"I'm sorry, girls," Ms. Workman said. "I should have listened. But you shouldn't have ruined my costumes. What am I going to do now? I have a float. But I have no one to ride on it."

"Let Cody and Maria ride," Diana said. "They fit your float theme—detectives, security, Sherlock Holmes. Their hats make great costumes."

"How about it, detectives?" Ms. Workman asked. "Will you do it?"

Cody and Maria smiled and climbed onto the float. They liked the solution to this mystery.

MYSTERY #9
The Case of the Purloined Pie

"Tomas," Cody said, "we think you took the pie. You said you went to get Mrs. Widen's mail. Everyone knows there's no mail delivery on Thanksgiving Day. Your alibi can't be true."

"When Jason left, you were alone with the pie," Maria took over. "Mrs. Widen was next door. And Maya was at home. You had a chance to take the pie without anyone seeing you."

"What do you have to say about this?" Cody asked.

Tomas took a deep breath "I didn't take it for myself. I took it for Mrs. Tripper. She fell and broke her arm yesterday. She couldn't make dinner for her family. I felt sorry for her.

"I wanted to do something for her. But I couldn't think of anything—until I saw your pies. I'm sorry."

"I'm sorry too," Mrs. Widen said. "Admitting your mistake is fine. But you'll need to pay for it too."

"How?" Tomas asked. "I don't have any money."

"You can help me bake a new pie," Mrs. Widen said.

"We'll all help," Maria said. "Anyone can make a mistake. Tomas was just trying to do a good deed. But he went about it the wrong way."

"I'll tell you what," Mrs. Widen said. "We'll make two new pies. We'll deliver three. Then we'll share the extra one."

"Good idea," Cody said. "I love pumpkin pie. It's just one more thing I'm thankful for."

MYSTERY #10

The Case of the Cherry Chocolate

"We think Mark spilled the chocolate," Cody said. "Mark said he heard the kitchen faucet dripping. But the TV is too loud. He couldn't have heard water dripping in the kitchen. We don't think he's telling the truth."

Mark's cheeks burned. "You're right," Mark said. "I spilled the chocolate. But I didn't do it on purpose. I came to the kitchen for a drink. The fudge smelled so good. I wanted to give it a stir. But I accidentally spilled it."

"Accidents happen," Mrs. Noel said. "I can make more fudge. But I wish you would have just told me what happened."

"I was afraid you wouldn't let me wrap candy anymore," Mark said. "I planned to use the money I earned to buy Christmas presents for my family."

"You can keep wrapping candy for me," Mrs. Noel said. "As long as you help me clean up this mess."

"We'll help too," Ling said.

"Right," Lisa agreed.

"Cody and I can help too," Maria offered.

Cody was still wondering how to get himself a taste of that fudge.